This Walker book belongs to:

_____

_____

_____

For Geraldine, Joe, Naomi, Eddie, Laura and Isaac
M.R.

For Elaine, Charlotte and Nicola
A.R.

First published 1990 by Walker Books Ltd
87 Vauxhall Walk
London SE11 5HJ

This edition published 2003

16 18 20 19 17 15

Text © 1990 Michael Rosen
Illustrations © 1990 Arthur Robins

The right of Michael Rosen and Arthur Robins
to be identified as author and illustrator respectively of this work
has been asserted by them in accordance
with the Copyright, Designs and Patents Act 1988

This book has been typeset in New Century Schoolbook

Printed in China

British Library Cataloguing in Publication Data:
a catalogue record for this book
is available from the British Library.

ISBN 978-0-7445-9800-1

www.walker.co.uk

Little Rabbit Foo Foo

retold by
Michael Rosen

illustrated by
Arthur Robins

WALKER BOOKS
AND SUBSIDIARIES
LONDON • BOSTON • SYDNEY • AUCKLAND

Little Rabbit Foo Foo

riding through the forest,

scooping up the field mice

and bopping them on the head.

Down came the Good Fairy and said, "Little Rabbit Foo Foo, I don't like your attitude, scooping up the field mice and bopping them on the head. I'm going to give you three chances to change, and if you don't, I'm going to turn you into a goonie."

Little Rabbit Foo Foo
riding through the forest,

scooping up the wriggly worms
and bopping them on the head.

Down came the Good Fairy

and said, "Little Rabbit Foo Foo,
I don't like your attitude,
scooping up the wriggly worms
and bopping them on the head.
You've got two chances to change,
and if you don't, I'm going to
turn you into a goonie."

Little Rabbit Foo Foo
riding through the forest,
scooping up the tigers
and bopping them on the head.

Down came the Good Fairy
and said, "Little Rabbit Foo Foo,
I don't like your attitude,
scooping up the tigers
and bopping them on the head.

"You've got one chance left to change,
and if you don't, I'm going to
turn you into a goonie."

Little Rabbit Foo Foo
riding through the forest,
scooping up the goblins

and bopping them on the head.

Down came the Good Fairy
and said, "Little Rabbit Foo Foo,
I don't like your attitude,
scooping up the goblins
and bopping them on the head.

"You've got no chances left, so I'm
going to turn you into a goonie."

Other books by Michael Rosen

ISBN 978-0-7445-2323-2

ISBN 978-1-4063-3097-7

ISBN 978-1-4063-2602-4

ISBN 978-1-4063-1832-6

ISBN 978-1-4063-3836-2

ISBN 978-1-4063-2655-0

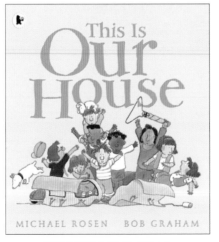

ISBN 978-1-4063-0564-7

Available from all good booksellers

www.walker.co.uk